Billy's Monster

Also by Pamela Sykes
Our Father!

Billy's Monster

by
Pamela Sykes

ILLUSTRATED BY
CAROLINE SHARP

THOMAS NELSON INC.

New York   Camden

Text copyright © 1968, 1971 by Pamela Sykes
Illustrations copyright © 1968, 1971 by
The Bodley Head Ltd.

First U.S. edition

Library of Congress Catalog Card Number: 73-160146
International Standard Book Number: 0-8407-6174-0
0-8407-6175-9 NLB
PRINTED IN THE UNITED STATES OF AMERICA

Contents

For
Richard

CHAPTER 1

Project

One day Mr. Betts, the headmaster, had news for the school. They were going to start a Natural History Museum. Everybody would help to collect things like old birds' nests, stones, fossils, pressed flowers, leaves, and skeletons of animals.

When all was ready, there would be a grand opening, to which parents would be invited.

When he came out of school, Billy was thinking so hard about the museum that he buttoned his sweater wrong and forgot his hat.

After he had put these things right, he had to run to catch up with Don, his older brother. Don was talking to his friend Henry.

"Skeletons would be the most exciting things to look for," he said.

"We would be lucky to find a complete one,"

said Henry, "but we might find some odd bones —or a skull."

"A skull?" said Billy, panting. "With crossbones, like on pirate flags?"

"Those are human skulls," said Don. "We won't find one of those."

"They'll be of little animals," Henry said. "Birds, rabbits. Perhaps a weasel."

"We must have a proper expedition," said Billy.

"What do you mean, 'we'?" said Don. "Henry and I are going to be the skeleton hunters."

"And me," said Billy.

"Skulls are most difficult things to find," said Don, "so big boys will have to do the searching."

"I'm big," said Billy. "Very nearly eight."

"We're ten," said Don, "so we'll do the skulls. You can look for fossils."

"I don't want to," said Billy.

"Wild flowers, then."

"The girls are doing that."

"Think of something you'd like to look for," said Don.

"I have," Billy said. "Skulls."

Henry had not been listening to any of this. He had been thinking. While he was thinking he had walked through a puddle, so that his shoes were wet and his legs splashed with mud. When Henry was thinking he never looked where he was going. When he was not thinking he was reading. Sometimes this could be useful.

"We'll have to dig," he said. "Quarry Wood would be a fine place."

"Why?" asked Don.

"Animals and birds often die in sheltered places," said Henry. "And there is soft earth up there under the trees."

"It's a bit dark for seeing," said Billy, who was not very fond of dark places.

"You won't be there," said Don.

Billy said nothing.

"I'll look up details," said Henry, "and tell you what I find out." He went off to his house, his head down.

"Making plans?" said Billy.

"You can just make your own," said Don.

At their gate, Bouncer leaped out to meet them. He was Billy's own dog, brown and white, and full of enthusiasm. When his tail wagged, all of him wagged.

Delighted to see the boys, Bouncer jumped up on Billy, tore around in small circles, snapped at a blowing leaf, missed, and fell into a rose bush. His nose was brown with wet earth.

"Bouncer is a very fine digger," said Billy.

Don said nothing.

At teatime, they told Mum and Dad about the museum.

"Henry and I are going to look for skeletons," said Don.

"And me," said Billy.

"Not you," said Don.

"Why not?" asked Mum.

"Skeletons are the most difficult things to find," Don explained. "So we older ones had better do it. We might borrow Bouncer, though. He does dig well."

"That's true," said Dad. "He's just dug up a row of young lettuce plants."

Bouncer, who had been listening, crept under the table.

"He didn't know he wasn't supposed to un-bury them," said Billy.

"He does now," said Dad. "I explained."

Billy held a small piece of bread and butter near his knees. A warm, wet mouth took it.

"He might be able to smell out skeletons," said Don.

"He's my dog," said Billy. "You can't have him."

"That's mean," said Don. "He'd like to come."

"So would I," said Billy, passing another mouthful under the table.

"You're feeding him. You're not supposed to," said Don.

"Oh, Billy!" said Mum.

"Tattletale!" cried Billy, red in the face.

"It seems to me," said Dad, "that this expedition had better be four strong. Don to lead, Henry to advise, Bouncer to dig, and Billy to do odd jobs."

"It seems to me like that too," said Billy.

"Oh, very well," said Don, "I suppose you'd better come, if Henry doesn't mind."

"He won't even notice," said Billy, "and he'll be pleased to have Bouncer."

Bouncer, hearing his name, came out from under the table licking his lips.

"No more," Mum told him. "You're not supposed to have snacks between meals."

"Especially after you've disgraced yourself," said Dad.

Billy thought it was time to take Bouncer for a long walk. In the fields he told him about the expedition. "You and I will have to dig like anything."

Bouncer sniffed a downy dandelion and sneezed.

CHAPTER 2

Expedition

Saturday morning was bright and blowy. Just the day for an expedition.

As leader, Don walked in front. Henry followed with a book called *A Guide to British Wild Life* under his arm. Billy came next, carrying the spade. Bouncer was supposed to be last, but he kept forgetting and scampering ahead.

Down the village street they went, past the post office, the blacksmith, the bus stop, and the Big House. Colonel Bluff, who owned it, was weeding his front garden. He stopped when he saw them and shouted, "Good morning—eh?"

"Good morning," replied three of the party. The fourth was pawing at a mouse hole in the hedge.

"Going on safari?" asked the Colonel, eyeing their belongings.

"Almost," said the leader. While he was telling the Colonel what they were doing, Billy whispered to Henry, "What's safari?"

"An expedition in the jungle, to hunt for wild animals, lions and tigers and things," said Henry. "The Colonel used to go on lots of safaris."

"I certainly did," said the Colonel, overhearing. "I can well remember . . ."

While he remembered, Billy thought longingly of jungles and wild animals. Tall grass, great snakes, screeching parrots. Much more fun than old Quarry Wood.

He sighed deeply.

On and on droned the Colonel. The boys listened politely.

Bouncer, who could not be expected to know about manners, yapped with impatience.

The Colonel stopped his story suddenly in the middle. "Bless my soul! How I do run on! I'm taking up your time."

The members of the expedition shuffled their feet awkwardly.

Bouncer barked again.

"Yes," said the Colonel. "The dog's right. You must be on your way. Got plenty of provisions?"

"No," said Billy.

"Must have provisions," said the Colonel. "Never heard of a safari without 'em." He raised his voice to a bellow, "Mrs. Maynard!"

Mrs. Maynard had looked after the Colonel's house for as long as anyone could remember. She was famous for her homemade cakes, always winning the baking contests at the local show.

When the boys heard her being called, they stopped shuffling and looked hopefully toward the house. An upstairs window opened and Mrs. Maynard's head appeared.

"Could we have provisions for a safari, please?" shouted the Colonel.

"How many?" called Mrs. Maynard.

"Three," answered the Colonel.

"Four," corrected Billy.

Don gave him a warning look.

"One is a quadruped," explained Henry.

Mrs. Maynard was seen to count the party. Bouncer barked again at just the right moment, so that he should not be missed.

Presently Mrs. Maynard bustled across the lawn. "Rock cakes, ginger cookies, bananas, and some chocolate," she said, handing them packages. "Luckily I was just cutting up the cold joint, so *this* is for the quadruped."

The last bundle evidently had a good smell for Bouncer. As it wafted over his head he stood on his hind legs and tiptoed along like a circus dog.

Thank-you's were said, the Colonel wished them good hunting, and the expedition moved off. Bouncer kept close to Henry.

Don took the rough path up to Quarry Wood. Because Henry was trying to read the book he was carrying, he fell over a stone, and the rock cakes rolled into the mud.

After they had picked the wettest parts of them off, it seemed a pity not to eat the remains.

The path was steep. Soon Billy lagged behind the others.

"Wait for me!" he called.

"You must be quicker," Don told him.

"It's the spade," Billy said. "It's taller than I am, which makes it hard to carry."

Don saw it was his duty to change loads. After that they climbed faster.

The trees in Quarry Wood were pine trees, very thick and dark. After the boys had walked into the wood for a few minutes, Billy looked around to make sure he could still see the way out. It would be a pity if the expedition were to get lost.

"I think we've come far enough," he said

soon, but the others went on until they found a soft spot.

"You can have first go with the spade," Don told Henry. "Billy can use the trowel."

"What about you?" Billy asked.

"I shall be foreman," said Don, "and inspect anything you find."

At first there was little to inspect—a number of pine cones, a plastic eggcup, and a hair clip. The diggers became excited when their tools struck something hard, but it was so often a root that they soon became discouraged.

"Your turn with the spade now," said Henry to the foreman.

"And you can have the trowel," said Billy.

"No, thank you," said Henry, "I'll inspect."

"But it's my turn not to have the trowel," Billy complained.

"Get on with it, young Billy."

Billy got on with it and discovered a white stone that Henry thought might be a flint. He spent so long considering it that Don became cross.

"We've got to get on!" he said. "I think this is a rotten place to—oh!"

Some small pale things lay on his heaped spade. They all crouched around.

Gently, Don uncovered a skull and several tiny bones.

"A bird," breathed Henry. "Quite large. A wood pigeon, perhaps." He wiped his fingers on his trousers and searched in his book for clues.

This seemed a good moment for provisions. When they unpacked them it was found that Bouncer had already helped himself to his share and was now cracking a large mutton bone under a tree.

"A fat lot of use he's turned out to be," said Don.

"Well, at least he's got a bone," said Billy. All the same, when there was nothing left to eat,

he went over to Bouncer and spoke sternly. "You're supposed to be digging."

Bouncer rolled his eyes and growled because he thought Billy was going to take away his bone.

"I don't want that old thing," said Billy. "We've got to dig for proper ones of our own."

But Bouncer was not in the mood for digging. He turned his back on Billy and made fierce lion noises.

Now there was a shout from Henry. He had found another small skull.

"A rabbit, I think," he said. "Or perhaps a squirrel. Where's my book?"

Don and Billy looked for the rest of the rabbit (or squirrel) but only found more roots—and a blister on Billy's thumb.

"Never mind," said Don at last. "We've got two good things—most of a bird and a skull. Not bad for one morning."

Billy thought it was very bad indeed. Neither he nor Bouncer had found anything at all. Nobody had said, "I told you so!" But he knew two people who were thinking it.

"Come on," said Don, kicking Henry gently. "It's time to go."

Henry, who had not felt the kick, went on reading, so Don and Billy packed the specimens carefully in the bag that had held the provisions and called to Bouncer, who was digging.

"Look," said Billy proudly. "He's got the idea at last!"

"About time," said Don. "Come on, Henry! You can do all that at home."

Henry stood up unwillingly. "It could be a weasel," he said.

Billy ran over to Bouncer. "What have you found, boy?"

Bouncer was too busy to hear. His nose was buried in a deep hole. His front paws scrabbled wildly.

"I do believe he's got on to something exciting," said Billy. Don came to watch.

"Good old Bouncer. Keep going!" he said.

Bouncer paused, sneezed, twitched his back half around, and dug again. Henry came over, still reading. A great shower of earth shot over him.

"Here!" he said to Bouncer. "Watch my book!"

The hole was so deep now that Bouncer was standing on his head. At last he came out of it panting, and wandered away to rest.

"There's nothing there," said Don, looking.

"There must be," said Billy.

"I can't think what would be buried so deep," said Henry. "Unless it was a prehistoric monster."

Bouncer returned. In his mouth were the well-chewed remains of his mutton bone. He dropped it carefully into his hole and began to scuffle the earth back.

"What a dog!" said Don. "He always gets things the wrong way around."

"This is a digging party, not a burying one," said Henry.

Bouncer finished his job and looked pleased with himself.

Don and Henry led the way back. Billy made Bouncer stay behind with him.

"It was bad enough when I didn't find anything," he said reproachfully. "You didn't have to make it worse by doing things backward."

Bouncer snapped at a waving leaf, not listening.

"We've got to do something to show them," said Billy with determination. "To jolly well *show* them!"

CHAPTER 3

Private Search

The next day, Don went to Henry's house to help him clean and label their bones.

Billy went for a long walk. He took Bouncer with him, as well as a picnic, a knapsack, and a trowel.

"You're not to make too much noise," he told Bouncer on the way. "This is a private safari—very private."

Bouncer didn't care. He squirmed and jumped and ran ahead of Billy down the village road past the Colonel's house and up the path to the woods.

At the beginning of the trees, Billy paused. Only a little light filtered between the close branches of the pines, and the wood seemed very big. Perhaps he would have changed his

mind if Bouncer had not suddenly remembered something important, and rushed ahead into the undergrowth.

"Come back!" called Billy, but Bouncer raced on. Billy hurried after him. Two are better than one in a dark wood.

By the time he had caught up with him, Bouncer had unearthed his precious bone and was playing with it. He threw it up and caught it and looked at Billy sideways, growling.

"Oh, do leave that silly bone!" said Billy. "We've got to find something ourselves today." He prodded the ground energetically with the trowel.

Something scampered through the undergrowth. It sounded rather large. Bouncer dropped his bone and stood with his ears cocked.

"It can't be anything very exciting," Billy said. "Foxes and deer are the biggest wild animals left in England. Dad said so."

When there was another scamper, closer and much louder, Billy hoped very much that Dad was right. At one time, long, long ago, there had been bears and wolves in England. Not many people came to Quarry Wood. Perhaps one or two bears might possibly still be lurking there?

"Don't be silly, Bouncer," said Billy. "Probably only a rabbit."

All the same, the more he tried not to hear the rustles and crackles around him, the louder they sounded. He found himself thinking less of the things he was looking for than of tall furry shapes lumbering on hind legs through the bushes and fierce bright eyes peering silently at him from between tree trunks.

"There's not enough light here," said Billy. "Let's go to the quarry."

The quarry lay along one side of the wood and was not really a quarry any more. At one time the place had been filled to the top with rubbish by local garbage trucks. Now they took their rubbish elsewhere and the quarry had become a lumpy open space where rosebay willow herb grew in summer and blackberries could be found in the autumn.

It was certainly lighter here, but though he dug and dug, Billy had no luck. The blister on his thumb burst and his back ached, but he could not bear to go home without anything. Bouncer lay down and went to sleep.

It was while Billy was eating his picnic (egg sandwiches, fruit cake, and an apple) that Bouncer woke up and started sniffing around on his own. Billy knew he was only looking for a new place to bury his bone, so he paid little attention.

Perhaps he ought to collect some leaves for the museum after all, he was thinking, or seeds. Or even some flowers that he could press.

Then he saw that Bouncer had made a new hole and was getting cross with it. He scratched this way and that, but it seemed to be growing no deeper.

"Poor old boy," said Billy. "Shall I help you?"

Bouncer was becoming frantic. Earth flew in every direction. The hold grew wider and wider. But no deeper.

There was something hard at the bottom.

"Let me look," said Billy. He pushed Bouncer out of the way and lay on his stomach, so that his chin hung over the edge of the hole.

He tapped the bottom. The trowel met something hard.

"It's a stone," said Billy. "I'll see if I can move it."

He worked away at uncovering the stone. Bouncer waited, watching.

"It's a huge stone," said Billy. "It goes downward." He scooped earth from all around its edges.

"I don't think I can move it," he panted presently. "It's too big." But he went on scrabbling, because by now he wanted to see what kind of a stone this could be that was so smooth and oddly curved.

He found a hollow on one side, then a matching hollow on the other. Then Bouncer jumped with all his feet into the hole, taking a great deal of earth with him.

"Get out of the way!" said Billy. "Your tail's waving in my face."

But Bouncer thought it was his turn, so Billy let him have it. Soon the hole was so big that there was now room for both of them to get into it.

They became very hot and excited as the extraordinary thing at the bottom of the hole was slowly uncovered.

Billy tapped it several times with the trowel and listened carefully.

"I don't believe it's a stone at all," he said.

He licked his finger, rubbed a patch of the thing free from earth, and frowned.

Then he stood up, got out of the hole, and walked all around it, looking downward.

A quite extraordinary idea came into his head. He tried to put it out again, but the idea stayed. He was almost sure he knew what the thing was made of. Also, the domed top and hollows and the shape reminded him strangely of the pictures in Henry's book.

Pictures of skulls.

But this thing was huge. Nearly three feet long. Gigantic. Monstrous.

Billy stared at it.

It couldn't be. It *couldn't be*.

But it was.

The skull of a Monster.

CHAPTER 4

The Secret

"Bouncer," said Billy in a voice that quavered a little, "I think it's time to go home."

For if this was a Monster's skull, it must have belonged to a Monster. And if a Monster had once lived in Quarry Wood, might not others still be lurking there?

On the other hand, it was important that nobody else should find the skull. Billy quickly shoveled earth over it and then spread branches over the place.

Some handfuls of grass and leaves made a good top covering. Now you could not tell there was a hole there. Billy grabbed the trowel and rucksack and ran, with Bouncer leaping along beside him.

The wood seemed darker than ever. Billy

looked neither right nor left as he ran. A pair of wood pigeons clattering suddenly out of branches over his head made him jump so much that his bumping heart was louder than any other noise.

They scurried clear of the wood at last. As they scrambled down the path, Billy dared to look back over his shoulder. The trees stood still and silent. No monstrous shape was following them. He slowed down a little.

By the time he reached home he had stopped panting, and his heart was more itself.

Mum met him in the kitchen. "Did you have a good time? Just look at Bouncer's face! Where have you been?"

"Around and about," said Billy. "He was digging."

"So I see. He's filthy. And his paws! Give him a good rubdown while you tell me about your walk."

Billy did his best to clean the dirt off Bouncer

and not to answer Mum's questions at the same time.

"You still haven't told me what you've been doing to get in such a state," she said. "Look at your hands!"

Billy looked at them.

"And your knees!"

They were worse. Billy escaped into the garden.

This turned out to be a mistake, for Dad was there. The first thing he said was, "Do you know anything about my trowel?"

"Er. Um," said Billy.

"I don't mind you borrowing things," said Dad, "if you ask first."

"I'm sorry," said Billy, going to fetch the trowel.

Don came home with his bird's bones neatly arranged in a flat box on cotton. "Skeleton of a pigeon or ring dove" said the label, and, in brackets, "some missing."

"Most missing, if you ask me," said Billy.

"I didn't," said Don.

"Get ready for dinner, please," said Mum.

The meal was quiet. Mum thought her own thoughts. Dad, Billy guessed, was thinking about people who borrowed things. Don thought how pleased Mr. Betts would be with his skeleton.

Billy thought about his Monster.

He thought about it after eating, and on the stairs, and in the bath while he was scrubbing his knees with the brush.

Don, cleaning his teeth, said through the foam, "What's the matter with you, young Billy?"

"Nothing," said Billy.

Half of him longed to tell Don about the Monster, but the other half would not let him. Don and Henry had said he was too young to hunt for skeletons. Flowers, they'd suggested, like the girls. Bouncer was too silly to dig, they'd said.

The Monster was a huge and unbelievable secret.

In bed he shut his eyes and thought about it, lying so large and mysterious under the earth. Clever old Bouncer to find it. Tomorrow after school they would go and look at it again. He remembered how dark and crackly the wood had been and thought perhaps they would go the day after.

Then he realized that the things for the museum had to be taken to school on Friday morning. How could he possibly manage the skull by himself? He would never even get it out of the hole! He would have to tell Don.

But if he accepted help, it would not be *his* Monster anymore; it would belong to all of them. Life could be very difficult.

When at last he fell asleep, he dreamed he was quite alone in the wood. There came a tremendous roaring, and through the trees lurched a huge and terrible creature that was rather like a bear, and rather like a wolf, and rather like a dinosaur. It had teeth as big as meat dishes and it clashed them at Billy.

"N-n-n-o!" said Billy in his dream. "You've got to come to school with me on Friday!"

At that the Monster roared more dreadfully than ever.

Billy-in-bed knew this was only the brown-and-white cow in the nearby field, but Billy-in-the-dream knew it was the noise angry prehistoric monsters made before they ate people.

He woke in a terrible shuddering fright and did not dare go to sleep again.

By now he was quite sure of one thing. He would tell Don and Henry about the Monster and if they wanted to part-own it, they were welcome to their share.

Having made up his mind, he could not wait to tell Don. He woke him much too early.

"Go away," said Don. He opened one eye and saw the gray dawn light. "It's night," he said angrily.

"No, no!" said Billy. "It's nearly time to get up."

Don burrowed far down into his bed.

Billy knew he was taking a risk, but by this time he didn't care. He pulled up Don's blanket from the bottom of the bed.

"Listen!" he hissed into the space between the sheets. "I've got a whopping great secret to tell you. Honestly. No one else knows. You *must* listen."

After a long time, Don did.

At first he simply did not believe Billy.

"Three feet long? You're making it up!"

"I'm not! I'm not! I'll show you."

"And Henry?"

"Yes. And Henry. But you mustn't tell anyone else."

"I should hope not. They'd think we were

nuts. Sure you're not trying to be funny?"

After his horrible dreams Billy was not at all in the mood to be funny. Don told Henry during recess. Billy saw them both looking at him, and whispering.

At lunchtime Henry said, "This is not a hoax?"

"No," said Billy. "I'll show you this evening."

So after tea the expedition of four again found itself in Quarry Wood.

"This way," said Billy. He was leader now. It was comforting to have people behind you, he found. He began to feel quite brave.

They reached the quarry and the useless empty holes Billy had made with Dad's trowel.

"Here, I think," said Billy, pushing through some briars. "No . . . here."

Henry fell into a blackberry bush and Don began to look suspicious.

"Look here, young Billy—"

"I *am* looking. Like anything. The trouble is

I hid the place so well."

Bouncer was tearing around in circles. "Why don't you help?" said Billy. "It was your hole."

Bouncer pounced on an imaginary mouse.

At last Billy found he was standing right over the place. The others helped him move the grass and leaves and branches. Then they scooped away the earth. Bits of something pale began to show through.

"There it is," said Billy.

"There's certainly something," said Henry.

Bouncer landed right on top of the something and was thrown out.

"It's his hole, really," Billy reminded the others.

"Can't help that," said Don, grunting as he

worked. "We've got to be able to see—I say, Henry!"

Don sat back on his knees and Henry stared into the hole. His eyes became round. His mouth fell open.

"It *is* a skull!" he said. "No doubt of it. Look, cranium, eye sockets—"

"But what is it the skull of?" said Don.

"A Monster," said Billy. "A prehistoric Monster. I told you."

"You know, young Billy," said Henry slowly, "I really think you might be right."

CHAPTER 5

Midnight Adventure

"Once we get it out, we'll be all right," said Henry.

"Think of getting it down that path from the wood, though," said Don.

"In the dark," added Billy.

They were in Billy's Dad's garden shed making plans. It had been agreed that this wonderful find must be kept a secret till Friday morning, when they would astonish everyone with it. This would mean transporting the skull from its hole in the dead of night.

Billy was glad that he had confided in the others. He could never have managed the operation by himself. Also, being able to talk about the Monster made it less frightening.

All the same, the idea of Quarry Wood at

night sent shivers down his back each time he thought of it.

He thought of it now.

Bouncer, dozing at his feet, stirred, and Don said, "What's the matter, young Billy?"

"Are you sure it wouldn't be better to get Mr. Betts to come up and see it in its hole?"

The others were shocked. "And miss their faces when we arrive?" said Don.

"I should have thought you'd have been keenest," said Henry, "considering it was your find."

"Bouncer's and mine," Billy said. "We did the finding, so you can do the fetching," he added hopefully.

"That's enough of that," said Don. "You can do your bit. Now let's make a list of what we'll need."

It was a long list. Spades and trowels to lever up the skull. Henry's homemade cart to put it on. Sacks to pad it, ropes to tie it. Flashlights.

"The cart will make a fearful noise coming down the road in the middle of the night," said Billy.

"Good man. Rags to muffle the wheels," said Don, writing.

The expedition was timed for the next night. Henry said there would be a full moon, which cheered Billy slightly.

"We must wear masses of clothes," said Don. "Just in case the mums find out."

"They'll be wild if they do," said Billy.

"All in the interests of science," said Henry.

"They might not see it that way," said Don. "You know how they're always thinking of dry shoes and clean nails instead of the things that matter."

By bedtime the next night all preparations had been made. They were to meet at midnight at the foot of the path. Don and Billy would bring the ropes and tools. Henry would have his trolley, ready muffled.

Billy thought they would never get to sleep. He listened to the television music from downstairs, kitchen sounds as last drinks were made, Mum and Dad talking on the stairs, their bedroom door closing.

Presently the yellow square of light on the tall garden fence vanished, which meant they had gone to sleep. A faint gray light hung over the garden. This would be the full moon Henry had promised.

It seemed hours before Don appeared. "Come on! It's ten to twelve."

Billy scrambled out of bed, shuddering. His clothes didn't want to go on him. The stairs whined as they crept down them. They let themselves out of the front door, so as not to wake Bouncer in the kitchen. It seemed a shame that he should be left out of the adventure, but even Billy agreed he would not have been a help.

The air was cold, the road silver, the hedges and houses black.

Henry was one more black shape. The church clock began to strike as they saw him.

Billy turned on his flashlight as soon as they started up the path to the wood.

"Switch it off and save the battery," Don said. "We'll need it later."

"There aren't any Monsters, there aren't any Monsters, there aren't any Monsters," Billy told himself as they entered the wood.

A big gray shape swooped silently across Don's path. He stopped with a gasp. Henry ran into the back of him.

"Get on," he said.

"D-didn't you see it?" Even Don's voice wobbled a little.

"No," said Henry. "And I didn't hear anything either, so it was probably an owl. They fly silently."

"Only an owl, only an owl," said Billy to himself. They reached the quarry, the cart bumping behind them.

This time they found the place easily because they had marked it with a big stick. They moved the covering layers and dug a trough all around the enormous skull.

"Now," said Don.

They all seized bits of it and pulled. It did not move.

"No good," said Henry. "We'll have to get the ropes under it."

The ropes were skipping ropes and the handles got in the way as they passed them under the skull. A long sad cry rose from the wood behind them.

"That old owl again," said Henry.

"I thought it was," said Don.

Billy hoped they couldn't hear his teeth chattering. What sort of a noise would a Monster make?

"Now," said Henry, "take the handles and *pull!*"

They pulled. The gigantic, pale thing, glimmering in the hole, rocked and resettled.

"Probably the first time it's moved in millions of years," said Henry.

Next time it tilted and came halfway out of its hole before falling back with a loud *thud*.

"Who would have thought it would be so heavy?" gasped Henry.

"What must the rest of it be like?" said Don. "If this is the head, the backbone and legs and things must be enormous."

"And we must be sitting on it," said Billy, not caring for the idea.

"Tell you one thing," said Don. "If it turns out that there's miles more of this creature, the whole class can come and dig it out. Now, are we ready for a last effort?"

Everybody clutched the rope handles.

"One," said Don. "Two—three—heave!"

They heaved and hauled and struggled and gasped, and inch by inch the gigantic thing rose higher and higher until at last it toppled out almost on top of Henry.

"Gosh!" he said, gazing at it in awe.

Billy said carelessly, "It wasn't a bad find, was it?"

Henry was already considering how best to load this trophy onto the cart. "We must get its center of gravity right," he said.

"What's its center of gravity?" asked Billy, but nobody told him, for the others were already getting ready for more lifting.

The skull seemed less heavy once it was on their own level, and quite soon it was on the cart and roped securely.

Henry studied it. "I'm not sure about the center of gravity."

"Oh, bother it!" said Don. He was thinking what Dad would say if he discovered two empty beds. Billy was thinking longingly of his own bed and wishing he were safely back in it. Henry was urged to stop fussing, and they set off.

It was much more difficult to drag the cart now. Being heavily laden, its wheels sank into the earth and proved difficult to steer. It kept jolting into trees and jamming against invisible roots.

By the time they reached the top of the path everyone was rather hot and cross. As soon as they started downward the cart banged into the backs of their legs.

"It's no good," said Don. "We must let it go on ahead."

This worked better, until the path took a sudden twist. Then the cart began to have ideas of its own. First it gained speed, so that they had to stumble after it. Then it began to tilt.

"Hang on!" cried Don, forgetting to be quiet.

But the rope had been wrenched from Billy's hands.

"Don't let go!" shouted Don, as Henry was flung to the ground.

Too late. Unable to hold the weight of the

cart by himself, Don was tugged helplessly after it.

Billy and Henry stood horrified as their leader, and the cart with its precious cargo, crashed together into the hedge.

CHAPTER 6

Big Moment

Billy and Henry plunged to the rescue.

"Are you all right, Don?" asked Billy.

"I would be if only you'd come and get me out!" said Don crossly. "I'm underneath the Monster."

"I said the center of gravity wasn't right—" began Henry.

"Oh, shut up about your old center of gravity. Give me a hand."

Billy and Henry between them righted the trolley and hauled Don from beneath it.

"I wonder if it's damaged," said Henry anxiously, inspecting the skull.

"It!" said Don. "What about me?" He hobbled a few paces. "I *think* I can walk. But I should think I've got about a million nettle stings."

Henry was retying the ropes. "If only we'd taken more trouble—"

"If only you hadn't let go—" said Don.

After reloading and retying, they began again, more slowly. The cart still seemed to want to dash into first one hedge and then the other, but this time they were ready for its sudden jerks, and the road was safely reached.

"Now we've got to be quiet," Don reminded the others.

Glad of the muffled wheels, they trundled the trolley and its extraordinary load down the silent street and into Billy's Dad's garden shed.

"Put it in the far corner," Don whispered.

They covered their treasure carefully with an old sheet. Henry breathed good-night." Don and Billy heard his footsteps stumble as he went on his way home, thinking.

Then they let themselves into the house. All went well till they reached the stairs. Then a small inquiring *woof!* came from the kitchen.

They stopped, quite still, holding their breaths.

The next little bark was drowsier. Then came the stirring noises of a body turning around and around in a basket. Then silence.

They waited in the blackness until they were sure Bouncer was asleep again. Then they tip-toed up to bed.

At breakfast Dad said, "I thought I heard Bouncer in the night."

"Not like him to be disturbed," said Mum. "Perhaps there was a fox in the garden."

The words, "No, but there's a Monster in the shed!" almost burst out of Billy. He stirred his tea fiercely.

Later, while they were searching for lost homework, Mum asked, "Have either of you boys been out before breakfast?"

"No!" they said together. You couldn't

count the middle of the night as before breakfast.

"Funny," said Mum. "There's a lot of mud on the stairs. Quite damp, too."

Billy looked at Don. Don searched busily through his satchel. "Time to go, young Billy," he said. And they went.

On the way to school Henry joined them. They told him the secret was still safe.

"When are we going to tell Mum and Dad?" Billy wanted to know.

"Friday morning," Don said. "Not a minute before. Don't forget, Billy."

"It's me," said Billy, with dignity, "who's kept the secret longest."

People were beginning to bring things to school for the museum—a robin's nest, a fossil, an old snakeskin, a collection of seashells. Tom brought a white sheep's skull. Everyone crowded around it, admiring.

"I bet it's the best skull we get," said Tom.

"Is it really natural history?" someone wanted to know.

"Of course," said Tom. "It's natural, isn't it? So it's natural history."

"But not *wild* life," said the same voice.

"It might have been a wild sheep," said Tom. But everyone knew his father was a butcher. "Anyway," he said, "it'll be the biggest."

It was terribly difficult not to say anything. Don looked at Henry. Henry looked at Billy.

"What about hopscotch, anyone?" said Billy.

At last Friday morning came. Henry came early. Don called Mum and Dad. "Come and see what we have in the shed!"

"I'm just doing the dishes," said Mum. "Couldn't you bring it here?"

"Yes, do that," said Dad, taking a quick look at the newspaper before he left for work.

"All right," said Billy. "We will."

They dragged the cart from the shed and trundled it around to the kitchen window.

"Do look! Look *now!*" shouted Billy.

Two faces appeared at the steamy window.

"One, two—three!" cried Don. They flung off the sheet.

There in all its glory was the Monster.

"What on earth . . . ?" began Dad. He came out of the back door. Mum followed him, her eyes wide. "Where did you get that thing?"

"Bouncer and I found it!" cried Billy.

Bouncer, hearing his name, galloped out of the kitchen, where he'd been helping himself to bacon rind. When he saw the Monster he leaped about yelping.

"Shut up, Bouncer!" said Don.

By the time three excited voices and one barking one had tried to tell the story, Mum and Dad, though still amazed, were not much wiser.

Dad said, "I think Mr. Betts is getting more than he bargained for," and laughed. But he was very interested, too.

Mum said, "I do hope you haven't done anything wrong by digging it up."

She watched the proud procession start off.
Billy led this time, hauling in front on the longest rope, to show that this was his find. Don
and Henry went on each side of him.

Bouncer capered along behind "by mistake
on purpose." They had not the heart to send
him home.

"After all, he found it. He must be there for the Big Moment," said Billy.

Now that the rags were off the wheels, the cart made a fine rattle. People came to gates, leaned out of windows, and called from doorways.

"Whatever have you got there?"

"A Monster," Billy shouted back happily.

Children on their way to school gazed in wonder, and ran beside them to see better.

"A Monster!" they shouted. The word got around. "Billy's got a Monster!"

Hands pointed up and down the road.

"But what is it?" Henry, the expert, was asked again and again.

"You'll have to ask Billy," said Henry. "He found it."

As they neared the school, a row of heads popped over the playground wall. Eyes stared. Voices shrieked.

"What have you got there?"

"A Monster!" called Billy, red and beaming.

The children poured from the playground to meet and join the procession.

Bouncer, who loved nothing more than noises and crowds, turned somersaults of joy.

Mr. Betts, in the school hall, heard the noise.

"What can that commotion be?" he asked the other teachers.

None of them knew.

"We'd better go and see," said Mr. Betts, leading the way.

The school building was quiet, for the classrooms and the playground were empty.

But there was a tremendous noise in the road —rattling and shouting and barking.

"Dear me," said Mr. Betts. "This will never do—"

He got no further, for before he could go on, he saw an extraordinary sight.

Coming in at the school gate, crimson with pride, was Billy. Don and Henry were helping him to drag what looked like a homemade cart. And on the cart—Mr. Betts stared and stared.

His other pupils, making a most disgraceful noise, burst through the gate. The three bearers, who seemed to have with them an ill-trained dog, hauled the cart right up to Mr. Betts and stopped, panting.

"What," asked Mr. Betts, almost too astonished to say anything at all, "is all this about?"

"Please, sir," said Billy, "it's my thing for the Natural History Museum. I found it—or rather Bouncer found it and I was there—and the others helped me get it back and cleaned it up so it's from all of us really, and we think it's a skull of a prehistoric Monster!"

There was a hush of amazement.

Then somebody said, "Who's got the biggest

skull now? This one's as big as an elephant."

Mr. Betts, after a startled closer look at the skull, spoke at last.

"The extraordinary thing is," he said, "that I think it *is* an elephant!"

CHAPTER 7

Triumph

"An elephant!" A buzz broke out.

"Where did you find this?" asked Mr. Betts.

"In the quarry!"

"The quarry!" More buzzing. Shorter people at the back of the crowd tried to push forward to see better. People in front did not want to move. Bouncer raced about.

"Whose dog is this?" demanded Mr. Betts.

"Mine, sir, please, sir," said Billy. "He found the Monster."

"Very commendable," said Mr. Betts. "But he's not being very helpful now. I must have quiet, *please!*"

When Mr. Betts spoke like that, everyone obeyed, even Bouncer. He wriggled to Billy's feet and sat on them.

71

"Now," said Mr. Betts, "let's hear the whole story."

"Well . . ." began Billy and Henry and Don.

"One at a time, please," said Mr. Betts. "Billy?"

"Well . . ." said Billy again, then stopped. The whole story? Then he thought—the midnight adventure was over now, nobody could eat them—and anyway he could not resist describing it. He took a deep breath. "We went off to look for skulls . . ."

Mr. Betts listened carefully. The other teachers listened. The children listened. Bouncer listened. Don and Henry listened for most of the time, butting in only a little toward the end.

"We had flashlights and boots and warm clothes . . ."

"It was the center of gravity that was the trouble . . ."

When the story was finished Mr. Betts said, "Hmm. Your parents may have something to say about some of your goings-on, but the co-operative effort of disinterring and transporting this—this—whatever-it-is—was certainly a most enterprising effort." The boys glowed. "As to positive identification, I will ring up a friend who is an expert on these things, and ask him to come and look at it.

"Meanwhile it had better go straight into the museum, and the rest of us must try to concentrate on lessons."

Of course nobody did. During history, a black car arrived and a bearded man went into the museum with Mr. Betts. They heard him come out and drive away. Everyone longed to know what he had said.

While the children were in school, the news swept around the village. As is often the case, it became slightly altered as it traveled. Billy had taken an enormous skull to school. Billy had taken an elephant's head. An escaped elephant had been seen in Quarry Wood. Billy had captured an elephant and chopped off its head to prove it.

When the postman told this to the Colonel, he looked pleased and said, "Ha! They had a good game then."

"This is not a game; it seems to be true," said the postman.

"Nonsense!" said the Colonel. "They were playing at safaris not a week ago, up in Quarry Wood. Told me themselves. Naturally they saw elephants. Lions and tigers, too, no doubt. Good game. Almost wish I'd gone with them, eh?"

At the same moment the milkman was talking to Mrs. Maynard at the back door.

"Great huge bone head," he said. "I saw it myself in the playground."

"I've seen plenty of them," said Mrs. Maynard with a sniff. "The Colonel used to bring them back from his trips and hang them on the walls. Horrible things."

"This was the size of an elephant," said the milkman.

"Very likely," said Mrs. Maynard. "Two pints, please. We used to have an elephant's head over the mantelpiece until I spoke my mind to the Colonel about spring-cleaning and he let me throw it out."

"They say Billy found this one himself," said the milkman.

"Where?"

"The old quarry."

"The quarry, you said?" Mrs. Maynard looked thoughtful.

Later she spoke to the Colonel. The Colonel said "Ha!" several times and chuckled. Then he went up to the quarry himself and poked about in the big open hole. He brought home a small metal label. It was bent and very rusty, but you could still read the writing: "Shot in India, 1935."

"That proves it," said the Colonel to Mrs.

Maynard. "What do we do now, eh? Seems a pity to spoil the fun."

But Mrs. Maynard said, "I hear there are experts being called in and no end of a fuss."

"Suppose I'd better ring Betts," said the Colonel. "Can't let the fellow go to all that trouble."

So the story was explained. The Monster was not prehistoric after all. The rest of it lay not under the nettles and brambles of the quarry but far away in India, where the Colonel had shot it.

Billy was enchanted. That his Monster was not prehistoric and mysterious worried him not at all. He much preferred to think the skull had belonged to a real elephant. An elephant that had actually lived in the steaming, screaming jungle.

Tom said, "I don't think it should be allowed to count. After all, it was only a bit of furniture of the Colonel's."

"Bit of furniture!" said Don. "It was quite the biggest, and one of the wildest, animals in the world in 1935. Better than your old sheep, any day."

Henry was bothered because he had not recognized the skull as an elephant's. "It was not having a trunk that was the trouble." He had at once borrowed a book from the library and discovered that elephants do not have bones in their trunks. He explained all this to Billy, who did not listen.

Now that his Monster was in no way shivery, he liked to think about it often, imagining the time when that skull had had a head around it and flappy ears and a trunk, not to mention a large body attached behind. The little piggy eyes would have seen snakes and parrots, poisonous flowers, and spiders as big as kittens. The great feet would have lumbered through swamps, swished through high elephant grass, and even trampled down mud huts if their owner was in the mood.

Parents were invited to the opening of the Natural History Museum. Four of them had had things to say about the midnight escapade, but that was over now. Everyone smiled.

The newly painted shelves and tables were covered with all the things people had brought. But by itself on the wall, in a place of honor, hung the skull that Don and Henry and Billy and many other people would always call the Monster.

SKULL OF A
MALE BABOON

Under it was a notice that said: "Skull of a male Indian Elephant, shot in India by Colonel Bluff, 1935. Rediscovered by Billy Smith, assisted by Don Smith and Henry Brown, in 1971."

Billy had Bouncer on a short lead. No one had actually said he could not bring him, so he hoped for the best. Bouncer tugged and choked and gasped with excitement.

Billy had a quick look at all the other exhibits to be polite. Then he took Bouncer over to see the great skull. "Look, boy! Our Monster."

He stayed, rooted before it, for the rest of the afternoon.

He thought he had never seen anything so magnificent in his whole life.